Bedtime

Rockpool Children's Books
15 North Street
Marton
Warwickshire
CV23 9RJ

First published in Great Britain by Rockpool Children's Books Ltd. 2008
Text and Illustrations copyright © Stuart Trotter / Design Concept Elaine Lonergan 2007
Stuart Trotter has asserted the moral rights
to be identified as the author and illustrator of this book.

A CIP catalogue record of this book is available
from the British Library.

Printed in China

rockpool
children's books

Stuart Trotter & Elaine Lonergan

Bedtime

'Hello, my
name is Rex...

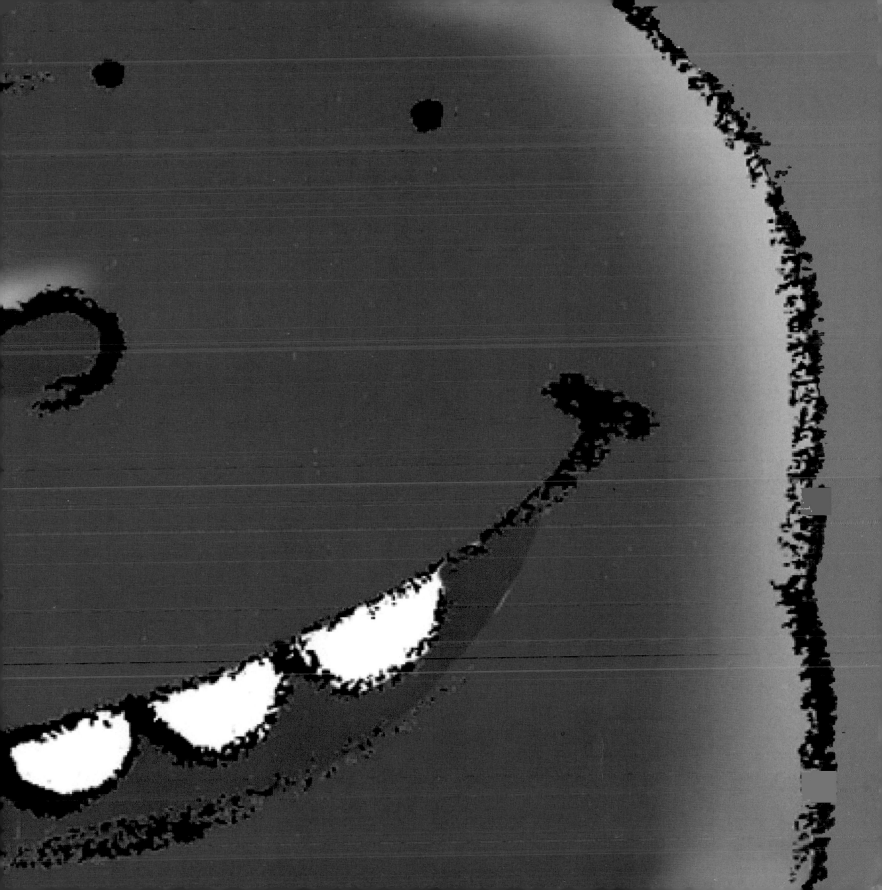

...and it's
time for bed!'

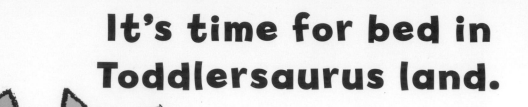

It's time for bed in Toddlersaurus land.

Lift the Flap

Everyone is getting ready to sleep.
But first...

It's time to sleep.

The ground is shaking, rumbling, quaking! What could it be?

Lift
the
Flap

No one else can get to sleep,
for someone is...

ROARING!

It's now sleepytime

in Toddlersaurus land,

and Rex is dreaming of

playtime in the morning....

but that's

another story!